School of Fish

Racing the Waves

By Jane Yolen

Illustrated by Mike Moran

Ready-to-Read

Simon Spotlight
New York London Toronto Sydney New Delhi

SIMON SPOTLIGHT
An imprint of Simon & Schuster Children's Publishing Division
1230 Avenue of the Americas, New York, New York 10020
This Simon Spotlight edition December 2019
Text copyright © 2019 by Jane Yolen
Illustrations copyright © 2019 by Mike Moran
All rights reserved, including the right of reproduction in whole or in part in any form.
SIMON SPOTLIGHT, READY-TO-READ, and colophon are registered trademarks of
Simon & Schuster, Inc.
For information about special discounts for bulk purchases, please contact
Simon & Schuster Special Sales at 1-866-506-1949 or business@simonandschuster.com.
Manufactured in the United States of America 1119 LAK
10 9 8 7 6 5 4 3 2 1
Library of Congress Cataloging-in-Publication Data
Names: Yolen, Jane, author. | Moran, Mike, illustrator.
Title: Racing the waves / Jane Yolen, Mike Moran.
Description: New York : Simon Spotlight, 2019. | Series: School of fish |
Summary: "A fish participates in a school field day"—Provided by publisher.
Identifiers: LCCN 2019023944 (print) | LCCN 2019023945 (eBook) |
ISBN 9781534453043 (paperback) | ISBN 9781534453050 (hardcover) |
ISBN 9781534453067 (eBook)
Subjects: CYAC: Stories in rhyme. | Fishes—Fiction. | Swimming—Fiction. |
Racing—Fiction. | Competition (Psychology)—Fiction. | Schools—Fiction.
Classification: LCC PZ8.3.Y76 Rac 2019 (print) | LCC PZ8.3.Y76 (eBook) |
DDC [E]—dc23
LC record available at https://lccn.loc.gov/2019023944

I'm silver. I'm cool.
I'm off to school.

I have my pack.

I have my snack
to eat before
we swim the track.

I stretch and practice
as I wait.
I hope the shark bus
won't be late.

Other fish
are stretching too.
Which team will win?
I don't have a clue.

I find my teammates.
We're five in all.
Some do the backstroke.
Some do the crawl.

We snack on the bus.
We give a high fin.
We worry about
which team will win.

I tell them, "Close your eyes, and then
take a deep breath.
Count to ten."

We do the count
and get to school.

We're mostly silver
and pretty cool.

Our swim coach greets us
at the track.
The lanes are lined
and painted black.

He tells us which teams
get set first.
We're on the outer lane—
the worst.

"Seems so much longer,"
says our Puffer.
Tuna adds,
"And looks much rougher."

Coach bubbles,
"Just swim fast,
and do your best.
Let fins and tails
do all the rest."

And then we hear the whale's
big blow.
Our fins are ready.
Coach shouts, "GO!"

We start forward fast.
There's a shout.
Fish teams from every school
head out!

My team zips fast,
a scorching pace.
Surely we are
in first place.

Up ahead,
or so I'm told,
the winning medals
gleam with gold.

I try to keep
my breath controlled.
When suddenly . . .

I look with dread.
How did that team
pull up ahead?

Their leader is—
it seems to me—
a sailfish,
fastest in the sea.

Feeling sad,
I start to slow,
but my best friend
calls out. "No!
Close your eyes,"
she says, "and then
take a deep breath.
Count to ten."

I do the count.
I wave a fin.
I'll lead our team
on to that win!

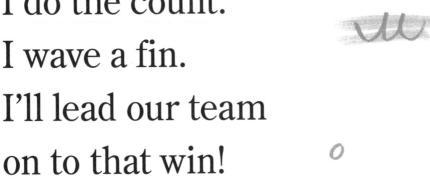

We swim real fast.
We feel real great
but finish just
a little late.

My best friend waves
a frantic fin.
We should be sad.
We didn't win.

But then I see her
grinning face.

"Second place!"
she shouts out.
"We have won *our* race."

Because
we medaled—
a first for our school.
Now we're all, all silver!
And we're *real* cool.